THE NEVER SINK NINE

Christy's
Magic Glove

BY GIBBS DAVIS

Illustrated by
George Ulrich

A BANTAM SKYLARK BOOK ®
NEW YORK · TORONTO · LONDON · SYDNEY · AUCKLAND

RL 2, 005–008

CHRISTY'S MAGIC GLOVE

A Bantam Skylark Book / June 1992

Skylark Books is a registered trademark of Bantam Books, a division of Bantam Doubleday Dell Publishing Group, Inc. Registered in U.S. Patent and Trademark Office and elsewhere.

ISBN 0-553-15988-7

Published simultaneously in the United States and Canada

Bantam Books are published by Bantam Books, a division of Bantam Doubleday Dell Publishing Group, Inc. Its trademark, consisting of the words "Bantam Books" and the portrayal of a rooster, is Registered in U.S. Patent and Trademark Office and in other countries. Marca Registrada. Bantam Books, 666 Fifth Avenue, New York, New York 10103.

PRINTED IN THE UNITED STATES OF AMERICA

CWO   0 9 8 7 6 5 4 3 2 1

*In memory of Ron Mutz, a true
Little Leaguer, who warned me
about the pleasures and perils of
baseball.*

Contents

CHAPTER ONE

Losing Isn't the End of the World

Walter Dodd squeezed into a booth at the Pizza Palace. "We blew it," he said as he threw his mitt on the table. "Move over," he said to Otis Hooper, the Never Sink Nine's catcher.

"*You* move over," Otis grunted. "I need more room than you do. I'm bigger and I weigh more."

Walter sighed and looked around the table at his Never Sink Nine teammates. After winning they always had fun eating pizza and talking about the game. But this Saturday they had lost for the first time and no one was hungry.

"Twelve to two," said Walter's best friend, Mike Lasky. "The Hawks creamed us." He blew a big bubble and popped it.

The whole team groaned.

Christy Chung stood up. "If Walter had been paying attention we would have won." She pointed at Walter. "*You* threw to the wrong base."

Walter's ears burned. "How would you know? You were doing ballet in the outfield!"

"No I wasn't!" shouted Christy.

"Were too!" said Walter.

Everyone started shouting.

Suddenly a loud whistle blew from across the Pizza Palace. Everyone stopped talking.

Grandpa Walt stomped over to their table. A whistle hung around his neck. He wore a sweatshirt with COACH across the front. Walter was proud of his grandfather. He was the only Rockville coach who had played minor-league baseball.

The Never Sink Nine sank down in their seats.

"No more blaming," said Grandpa Walt. "If anyone here played a perfect game today stand up and let's see you."

No one moved.

Walter looked down at his mitt. He *had* thrown to the wrong base once or twice. Everyone on the team had made mistakes.

"Even the best players goof up sometimes," said Grandpa Walt. "Anyone can be a good winner, but it takes guts to be a good loser. And no matter how good you are, you're going to lose sometimes."

"But we've won every game so far," said Christy. "Why'd we lose this one?"

Tony Pappas looked up from the picture he was drawing. "I can show you," he said. Tony drew pictures of all their games.

"Okay, Tony," said Grandpa Walt. "Show us."

Tony stuck his pencil behind one ear and held up a comic-strip drawing of today's game.

Everyone leaned forward to look. "Everyone did sort of dumb things today," Tony said.

3

"You all were walking around the bases, not running," said Grandpa Walt. "Even Homer slept through the game." He pointed through the window at their team mascot. A goat wearing a Never Sink Nine cap was tied to a parking meter. "You forgot to play as a team"—Grandpa Walt looked over at Walter and Otis and then at Christy and Melissa—"and we need to see more effort up the middle of the field."

"What does that mean?" Walter asked.

Grandpa Walt took a piece of Tony's drawing paper and drew a baseball diamond. He drew an arrow from home plate straight through to center field.

4

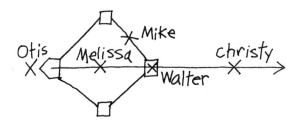

"All your positions are important," said Grandpa Walt, "but the most important thing is to keep your mind on what you're doing. Forget about the game we lost and start training for Saturday's game against the Vampires."

"I'm in training already," said Christy. "*Ballet* training. It's great for baseball."

Walter rolled his eyes.

"Ballet classes help me to concentrate," said Christy. She twirled in a straight line across the Pizza Palace.

The boys ignored her.

"A lot of athletes take dance lessons," said Melissa, frowning. She was their best pitcher.

5

"Not us," said Walter. "We're runners." The other boys nodded in agreement.

"We need magic to win," said Pete Santos. He waved his straw like a magic wand. Pete was a magician and loved to do magic tricks.

"My grandfather knows magic," said Christy. "I'll ask him for some."

"There's no magic to training," said Grandpa Walt. "It's just practice, practice, practice."

The team groaned.

"Cheer up, team," said Grandpa Walt. "Losing isn't the end of the world. Think about Saturday's game with the Vampires."

"What if we lose that game too?" said Felix.

"Then we'll train harder." Grandpa Walt wiped his mouth on a napkin. "But we'll still enjoy our pizza!"

He got out his car keys and headed for the door. "Never Sink Nine bus now loading!"

Everyone squeezed into Grandpa Walt's old station wagon for the ride home—except

6

Pete. He untied Homer, waved to his team-mates, and walked home with the team mascot.

Walter and Mike were the last to be dropped off. Grandpa Walt pulled up in front of Mike's house.

"See ya later, alligator," said Walter.

"In a while, crocodile." Mike grabbed his backpack and a book fell out. Walter handed it back to him.

"Did you find your missing library book yet?" asked Mike.

Walter shook his head. "No," he said.

"'Bye, sport." Grandpa Walt waved good-bye to Mike.

Walter had a sinking feeling in his stomach. This morning Mrs. Bumby, the school librarian, had warned him about his missing book. If he didn't find it by Friday he'd have to work in the library on Saturday. But if he had to work in the library he would miss the game!

Walter closed his eyes and tried for the hundredth time to remember where he'd left

7

the book. It was no use. He'd have to wait and try again tomorrow. After all, it was only Wednesday and there were two whole days before Saturday.

Walter opened the car door and grabbed his backpack. "You coming Friday for supper?" he asked Grandpa Walt.

"Don't I always?" said Grandpa Walt. He grinned and pulled down Walter's cap. "Go find your lost library book. It must be in there somewhere."

Walter ran toward his front door. Grandpa Walt was right. His book was bound to turn up.

CHAPTER TWO

The Magic Glove

The next morning Walter and Mike decided to begin training for Saturday's game. They jogged all the way to school.

"We made it," gasped Walter. He threw his backpack down on the grass in front of Eleanor Roosevelt Elementary School.

"I'm dyin'." Mike collapsed on the grass next to Walter. His tongue hung out of his mouth. "Water, water."

Walter pulled out his water pistol and squirted a stream into Mike's mouth.

"Thanks, partner." Mike wiped his mouth with his sleeve.

Melissa Nichols and her younger sister, Jenny, bicycled over to them. They looked down at Walter and Mike.

"What's wrong with you?" asked Melissa. "You look like you just ran a hundred miles."

"We're in training," said Walter. He tried doing a push-up and fell to the ground in a heap.

"Oh, really?" said Melissa with a laugh. "In training for what? Clown school?"

"If you want a *real* workout, Christy's giving a ballet class after school today," said Jenny.

Walter and Mike rolled their eyes as the girls locked their bikes and walked inside.

"Walter! Mike!"

Walter turned around. Otis Hooper shouted at them from their classroom window. "Hurry up. Come see Christy's magic glove!"

"I'll bet it's one of those expensive new ones from Swenson's," said Walter, heading for the door.

10

The Magic Glove

Swenson's Sporting Goods was Walter's favorite store in Rockville. He knew every inch of it with his eyes closed.

Inside Mrs. Howard's third grade classroom everyone was clustered around Christy's desk.

Walter pushed his way through the crowd. Christy was holding her baseball glove over one ear like a telephone.

"What's she doing?" said Mike.

"That's her same old mitt," said Walter. "What's the big deal?"

"Shhhhh!" said Pete. "Her glove's talking."

"Talking?" Walter and Mike looked at each other.

Christy slowly lowered her glove. She stared into space. They all held their breath. "Tomorrow it's going to rain," she said.

"Wow," said Otis. "That's what the weather forecast said. Your glove really must be magic!"

"You dummy," Walter said to Otis. "If you heard it was going to rain on the weather forecast, Christy heard it too."

11

"I did not," said Christy. "My magic glove told me." She held out her baseball glove. A small creature was painted inside the pocket. It held a baseball in one claw.

"Cool," said Mike. "It's a monster."

Christy jerked her glove back. "It's not a monster. It's a dragon. My grandfather's visiting from China and he painted it in my glove for good luck." She moved closer to Mike and whispered, "Dragons are magical. My dragon speaks to me."

Mrs. Howard leaned over them. Her daisy earrings almost touched Christy's baseball glove. "Everyone take your seat. It's time for class."

Mrs. Howard walked to the front of the room where a map of the world covered one bulletin board. She pointed to a large country in the Far East. "It seems you're all interested in China, so let's study it now."

Christy hugged her magic glove and smiled.

Mrs. Howard talked about China all morning. Walter didn't hear a word. He was daydreaming about pitching a no-hitter like Nolan Ryan. *They'll name a baseball field for me*, thought Walter. "The Walter P. Dodd field," he muttered to himself.

The recess bell rang. Everyone raced for the door.

Mike nudged Walter. "Earth to Walter, Earth to Walter. Wake up! We'll be the last ones to see the answer to Pete's joke!"

Walter looked up at the blackboard. Every day Pete Santos wrote a new joke on the board and left the answer in a different place. He read today's joke.

Pete's Joke of the day
Thursday
How can you tell that a
vampire likes baseball?

"Come on," said Mike, heading for the door. "Pete left the answer on the hall bulletin board!"

Walter followed Mike into the hallway. Their classmates were crowded under the bulletin board. Walter pushed his way to the front and read the answer:

Every night he turns into a bat.

Otis punched Walter in the arm and burst out laughing. "A bat, get it? Vampire bat, baseball bat!"

Walter laughed as hard as Otis.

Click, click, click, click.

Walter stopped breathing at the sound. He knew that Mrs. Bumby was coming up the hall. She was the only person in school whose high-heeled shoes made clicking noises on the floor.

"What's all that racket?" said Mrs. Bumby. "You're disturbing my students in the library."

"Sorry, Mrs. Bumby," Mike said. He and Walter turned and walked quietly toward the playground door.

"Mr. Dodd!"

Walter froze.

"Come back here, young man. I want to talk to you."

Walter turned around slowly and smiled weakly.

"Where is that missing library book?" Mrs. Bumby asked.

Walter shrugged. He felt his face turn red.

"This is the third time you've lost a book," said Mrs. Bumby. "Remember, if you don't find it you'll spend Saturday with me in the library. You'll value books more after a day of taking care of them. Meet me in the library Saturday, ten A.M. sharp."

Walter felt like crying. He couldn't miss the game. He *had* to find the book in time. He trudged out to the playground.

Christy was sitting on the grass watching Mike play catch with Felix. Walter looked at her glove. Could it really be magic?

Walter sat down next to Christy. He checked to make sure no one was listening. "Can your glove help *anyone?*" asked Walter.

"Sure," said Christy. "My glove will help us win Saturday's game against the Vampires. Only a dragon can beat a vampire."

Walter thought of Mrs. Bumby. She was scarier than any vampire.

"Can your glove help find lost things?" asked Walter. "Like, say . . . a library book?"

Christy frowned. "Losing a library book is pretty serious. I don't know." She cupped the glove to her ear like a seashell. After a few seconds she lowered the glove. "My dragon says, 'Learn to concentrate. Then you'll find it.'"

17

"How?"

"Do what I do." Christy sat cross-legged.

"What for?"

"It helps you think." Christy closed her eyes. She took a long, deep breath and blew it out very slowly. "Breathe like this and think hard, really hard, about your book."

Walter closed his eyes and took a long, deep breath. He thought about his book until his ears burned, but he couldn't remember where it was. His stomach growled. He opened his eyes. "It's time for lunch," he said.

Christy was disgusted. "Walter, you're dumb." She jumped up and twirled over to Melissa.

"Tomorrow I won't be this hungry," Walter said to himself. "I'll try again then."

CHAPTER THREE

In Training

After school on Friday Walter and Mike jogged into downtown Rockville for ice-cream cones. They ordered their favorite flavors—chocolate chip and bubble gum.

"We're gonna be in great shape for tomorrow's game." Walter collapsed on the front step of Wilson's Ice Cream Shop.

Mike licked his ice-cream cone. "Yeah, if we *make* it to Saturday."

"Grandpa Walt was right," said Walter. "We didn't concentrate at our last game." He crossed his legs and closed his eyes.

19

"What're you doing?" asked Mike.

"Thinking," said Walter. "Try it."

Mike crossed his legs and closed his eyes. "What should I think about?" he whispered.

"The Vampires game. Shhhh," said Walter.

"My cone is melting," whispered Mike.

Walter opened his eyes and sighed. Now he knew why Christy was so annoyed when he said he was hungry. He looked across the street at Chung's Restaurant. Grandpa Walt's apartment was above it.

"Come on," said Walter, crossing the street. "Maybe Grandpa Walt is home."

Walter pressed a buzzer beneath the Nameplate that read WALTER P. DODD. No one answered. A small message pad and a pencil dangled from a string below the card. Walter wrote:

See you tonight.
(also) Walter P. Dodd

20

In Training

Every Friday night Grandpa Walt had dinner at the Dodds'. Tonight Walter would ask Grandpa Walt to help find the missing book. It was his last chance before the game.

"Hey, look at this." Mike had his nose pressed up against the window at Chung's Restaurant. A sign on the window read: CLOSED UNTIL 5 P.M.

Walter looked through the window. Christy was standing in the middle of the restaurant dressed in tights and a leotard and her ballet shoes. Melissa, Jenny, Katie Kessler, and Otis were facing her. Christy was showing them her ballet warm-up exercises. The tables had been pushed to one side and the chairs were stacked up against the wall.

"What's *Otis* doing there?" said Walter.

"Traitor," muttered Mike. "He's supposed to be running with us."

"Let's sneak in," Walter said quietly.

Walter opened the door enough to slip through. A bell jingled above the door. Everyone turned around.

21

"Hurry up," Christy said to them. "You're late."

"We're not here to dance," said Walter. "We already ran three miles."

"Yeah," said Mike.

"You mean *crawled* three miles," said Melissa. "I saw you."

Everyone chuckled, including Otis.

Walter marched up to Otis. "What're *you* doing here?"

Otis turned pink. "Christy said ballet would help me lose weight."

"That's right," said Christy. "Otis has a lot of potential. With a little practice he could be a good dancer. Show them your plié, Otis."

Otis smiled and walked into the center of the room. He placed his heels together and bent his knees about twelve inches apart. His arms formed a perfect circle in front of him. The class clapped. Otis smiled from ear to ear.

"He looks like a human basketball hoop," said Walter.

"Bet *you* couldn't do that," said Christy.

Everybody looked at Walter and waited.

"Ballet's easy," Walter said, tossing down his backpack. He walked to the far end of the room. He tried to remember how Christy leapt through the air.

"Watch this," he said, taking a running start. He squatted and sprang as high as he could. He felt like he was flying and would never come down.

"Look out!" shouted Jenny.

Crash!

Walter landed in a pile of chairs. Otis and Melissa helped him up.

"Easy, huh?" said Christy.

Walter rubbed a sore spot on his arm. "That was just a practice jump," he mumbled.

Otis patted Walter on the back. "You looked pretty good until you crashed."

"Thanks," said Walter.

"We've finished our ballet lesson," said Katie. "What should we do now?"

"I know," said Melissa. "Let's spy on the Vampires."

23

"Their team sponsor, Costume Corner, is right down the street," said Christy, leading the way. "The kids wear really great costumes at all their games."

Everyone followed Christy down the street to the store on the corner. The window was painted with a vampire picture and a sign that read: COSTUME CORNER—KANGAROOS, KINGS, AND VAMPIRES!

Walter pressed his nose against the glass. A boy in a vampire cape was inside opening boxes of costumes.

"It's Johnny Crandall!" said Walter.

"No wonder he always has the best Halloween costume," said Mike.

Walter knocked on the window and waved at Johnny.

Johnny opened the door and covered his face with his cape. "Good afternoon, boys and ghouls. Enter." He lowered his cape and smiled. He wore a Vampire team shirt under his cape that read: COSTUME CORNER'S VAMPIRES. WE BITE.

24

"Wow," said Walter, walking inside. "This place is cool."

The store was filled with mannequins wearing different costumes. Mr. Crandall walked out from behind the counter.

"We just got some new costumes in," he said. "Want to try a few on?"

"Yeah!" everyone shouted.

Johnny put some costume boxes on the counter.

Walter put a pirate's black patch over one eye. "Look at me!" he shouted, holding a plastic sword. "I'm a pirate!"

Melissa slipped on a knight's helmet. "I'm a knight like Sir Lancelot."

They spent the rest of the afternoon trying on costumes and talking about Saturday's game.

"Why don't the Never Sink Nine come in costume too?" said Johnny. "They don't have to be anything fancy. You could make up your own costumes."

"That sounds like fun," said Melissa.

"We could have a costume party after the game at my parents' restaurant," added Christy.

Everyone agreed. When it was time to say good-bye Johnny waved at them from the door. "See you at the game tomorrow. Don't forget to dress up!"

"I'll either be Beethoven or a cop," said Mike. Mike played the piano, and his dad was a policeman. "What're you going to be?" he asked Walter.

"I don't know," said Walter.

Just ahead of them Walter spotted Mrs. Bumby coming out of the Book Nook. He hid behind Mike until she walked past. Walter sighed. "That was a close one."

"Haven't you found that book yet?" asked Mike.

Walter shook his head. "If I don't find it by tomorrow I have to work in the library during the game."

"You can't miss the game *and* the costume party," said Mike. "You've got to do something quick."

27

"Grandpa Walt is coming to dinner to-night," said Walter. "He'll help me find it."

Mike ran ahead of him. "Race you home!" he called back.

Walter ran after him. But his heart wasn't really in it.

CHAPTER FOUR

Detective Dodd

At dinner Walter was too worried to eat. He picked a cherry out of his pie and squashed it with his fork.

"What's wrong, Walter?" asked Mrs. Dodd. "Cherry pie is your favorite."

"Nothing, Mom," mumbled Walter.

"Nothing but a lost library book," said Walter's older brother, Danny, with a grin.

Walter shot Danny a dirty look.

Mr. Dodd frowned at Walter. "Didn't you lose a library book earlier this year?"

"*Two* books," said Danny.

29

Walter's ears burned. He kicked Danny under the table.

"Turkey brain," whispered Danny and kicked him back.

"Stop it, boys," said Mrs. Dodd.

"Maybe I can help," said Grandpa Walt. "What was the name of your book?"

"Encyclopedia Brown Tracks Them Down."

"Isn't he a boy detective?" asked Grandpa Walt.

Walter nodded. He loved mysteries, especially short ones. He was a slow reader.

"You know, all good detectives retrace their steps when they've lost something," said Grandpa Walt. "What do you say we play detective after dinner tonight?"

"Great!" Walter popped a squashed cherry in his mouth. He felt better already. Maybe Grandpa Walt could save him.

After dinner Grandpa Walt made a list of all the places Walter had been the day he lost his book:

1. House-bedroom, bathroom, kitchen
2. Grandpa Walt's car
3. Diamond Park—Willie Mays field

"Three places," said Grandpa Walt. "Let's start with the house. You look in your bedroom and the bathroom. I'll check out the kitchen."

Walter raced up the stairs to his bedroom. Danny was lying on his bed, reading.

"Did you see my book?" asked Walter.

"Do pigs fly?" Danny laughed at his own joke.

"Very funny." Walter searched under his bed and in his closet and drawers. He found half a candy bar, a broken yo-yo, and his old baseball mitt. He stepped across a line of tape that divided his side of the room from Danny's.

31

Danny peered over the top of his book. "Get back," he warned. "You're on *my* side."

"Pleeeeease," pleaded Walter. "I have to look *everywhere*. If I don't find my book I can't play tomorrow. Mrs. Bumby is going to make me work in the library."

Danny's face softened. "That's rough." He checked his watch. "Okay. You can have exactly five minutes. Go!"

"Thanks." Walter dove under Danny's bed. He checked every inch of both sides of the room.

"Any luck?" asked Danny.

Walter showed him a handful of dust balls and gum wrappers.

"Maybe Grandpa Walt found it," said Danny.

Walter looked hopeful. He raced down to the kitchen. Grandpa Walt was down on his hands and knees looking under the sink.

"No luck here," said Grandpa Walt. He got out his car keys and headed for the door.

"Let's try Diamond Park while it's still light outside."

Walter followed him out to the driveway. Together they searched the old station wagon. Grandpa Walt's coach whistle was under a car seat. Grandpa Walt blew it. "This car is as clean as a whistle," he said with a chuckle.

The sun was setting when they arrived at Diamond Park. They hurried over to the Willie Mays field. "You take the outfield, Detective Dodd," said Grandpa Walt. "I'll check the infield."

Walter searched every inch of the field. Finally it was too dark to see any more. He picked a blade of grass, held it between his thumbs, and blew hard. It sounded the way Walter felt—sad.

Grandpa Walt put an arm around Walter's shoulders as they walked back to the car. "Sorry, slugger. Looks like you're doing library duty tomorrow."

"It's just one game. There'll be lots

more," Grandpa Walt said when they reached the Dodds' driveway.

"I know," said Walter. But he didn't mean it. He wouldn't get to play with his friend Johnny Crandall and the Vampires. He wouldn't even get to wear a costume or go to the party afterward. Christy's magic hadn't worked. And Grandpa Walt hadn't fixed things.

Later that night Walter put on his lucky socks. Grandpa Walt had given them to him after the Never Sink Nine's first game. He stuffed his mitt with one of his baby teeth, a rabbit's foot, and his five lucky marbles.

"What're you doing?" asked Danny.

"I need all the luck I can get," said Walter.

"Forget about luck," said Danny. "You need a miracle." He turned out the light.

"Miracle, miracle, miracle, miracle, miracle," whispered Walter five times. Five was his lucky number. He shoved the bulging mitt under his pillow and yawned. It had been a long week. He was tired of hiding from Mrs.

Bumby and of trying to find his book. He looked up over his bed where his solar system mobile was hanging. Grandpa Walt had helped him make it for school.

Walter closed his eyes and started to dream. He imagined himself a major-league player on Saturn. He was at bat in the Solar System Play-Offs. Visitors from every planet were there cheering him on. "We love Walter! We love Walter!"

"I don't," said a voice. The catcher lifted her mask. It was Mrs. Bumby! She pointed at Walter. "*He* lost his library book."

The crowd gasped in horror.

The Saturn police dragged Walter off to be sentenced for his horrible crime. "No more baseball," said the judge.

"He's a good boy," Grandpa Walt begged the judge. "He *tried* to find the book."

"To jail!" shouted the judge. "Take away his mitt!"

"*No!*" cried Walter, waking up. He was hugging his mitt to his chest.

Danny was sitting on the bed beside him. "It's okay," he said. "You had a bad dream."

Walter sank back against his pillow. He looked around their room and sighed. He was definitely back on Earth.

"Ready to go back to sleep?" asked Danny, reaching for the lamp switch.

Walter shook his head. "Don't turn off the light!"

Danny, half asleep, looked down at Walter. Walter, wide awake, blinked back at him.

"How about a midnight snack?" said Danny. "Maybe there's some pie left." He started for the kitchen. "Come on, Walt. I haven't got all night. If you read awhile you'll fall asleep. You always eat when you read."

A light went on in Walter's head—a *refrigerator* light!

"That's it!" said Walter. "*I left my book in the fridge!*" He jumped out of bed and tore down the hall past Danny.

Walter remembered now. He had put his book on the refrigerator shelf while he made a sandwich.

Danny followed him into the kitchen. "What's going on?"

"My book's in here," said Walter, opening the refrigerator door.

The boys looked inside past heads of lettuce, cartons of milk, and mountains of leftovers.

No book. Not one page.

Danny patted Walter's shoulder. "At least there's some cherry pie left." He reached for the pie. Underneath was a paperback book pressed open to Chapter Three, "The Case of the Flying Submarine."

Walter's eyes popped open. "Look!" He grabbed the book before it could disappear again. "I guess I was too worried to notice when I put the leftovers back after dinner."

"Only a turkey brain like you would leave a book in the fridge in the first place." Danny

37

rumpled Walter's hair. "Looks like you may play the Vampires, after all."

After Walter and Danny finished the pie they went back to bed.

Walter read the rest of *Encyclopedia Brown Tracks Them Down* by flashlight under his blanket. By the time he finished the book was toasty warm in his hands.

Encyclopedia Brown was pretty smart, thought Walter, snuggling under his covers. He never gave up until he found what he was looking for. "Neither do I," Walter said to himself.

He wondered if Mrs. Bumby would still be angry when he gave her his library book in the morning.

CHAPTER FIVE

Lost and Found

Saturday morning Walter dressed for the Vampires game. It took a whole hour to put together a detective costume. He bicycled quickly to Eleanor Roosevelt Elementary and checked his Babe Ruth wristwatch: 9:44. He had exactly sixteen minutes to return his library book and get to Diamond Park.

Walter grabbed the Encyclopedia Brown book and raced down the empty hallway. He stopped to catch his breath and peeked in the library door. Mrs. Bumby was sitting behind her desk.

She's waiting for me, thought Walter. *What if she won't let me go to the game anyway?*

"Help, help, help, help, help," he whispered five times for good luck.

Walter stepped inside.

"Walter, is that you?" Mrs. Bumby peered at him over her glasses. She was frowning.

Walter had forgotten he was wearing his detective costume. He took off the sunglasses attached to his big plastic nose and mustache.

Mrs. Bumby's frown turned into a big grin.

"Help, help, help, help, help," Walter whispered again under his breath. He held out the Encyclopedia Brown book. "I found it." He put down his mitt and handed her the book.

Mrs. Bumby leafed through the book. She stopped at "The Case of the Flying Submarine." A small cherry-red spot stood out on the page.

"Hmmmm," Mrs. Bumby said. "Is cherry your favorite flavor? I hope you'll be more careful with books from now on." She looked at Walter in his father's trench coat and felt hat. "Is everyone on your team playing in costume?"

Walter nodded. "And the other team too."

Mrs. Bumby's face softened. "When I was your age my brother used to let me play on his team sometimes."

"*You* played baseball?" Walter tried to imagine Mrs. Bumby in a baseball uniform.

"It's a lovely game, isn't it?" said Mrs. Bumby, smiling.

Walter nodded. "Well . . .'bye." He turned to leave.

"Walter."

Walter froze. He turned around slowly.

"Catch!" Mrs. Bumby tossed Walter's mitt through the air. It landed in his hands. "Have fun!" she said.

"Thanks." Walter smiled shyly at Mrs. Bumby before he ran out the door. *Maybe she's not so bad after all,* he thought as he hopped on his bike. *I guess you can't judge a book by its cover,* he thought, and laughed out loud at his own joke. He'd have to pedal extra hard to make it to the game on time, but he didn't mind. The day was already turning out better than he'd expected.

CHAPTER SIX

The Vampires Game

Walter stopped his bike on the curb across from Diamond Park. He waited with Mrs. Miller, the traffic guard, for the light to change.

Mrs. Miller looked at Walter's costume. "Playing in the Vampires game?" she asked.

Walter nodded. "Do you know which field they're on?"

"Can't miss it." Mrs. Miller pointed toward the Babe Ruth field. "Only diamond with a vampire on the pitcher's mound."

The light changed and Mrs. Miller led Walter across the street.

"Thanks," said Walter, heading for the Babe Ruth field.

"Have fun, Walter!" shouted Mrs. Miller.

Walter bicycled past witches and monsters to the Never Sink Nine dugout. He barely recognized his teammates.

"Walter!" Mike waved a police captain's hat in the air. "I thought you couldn't play today!"

Christy and Melissa stepped out of the dugout in their ballerina and cowgirl costumes. Melissa held one of her toy horses.

"What about your missing library book?" asked Christy.

"I found it," said Walter. "Mrs. Bumby said I could play."

Christy leaned toward Walter and whispered, "My dragon knew you'd find it if you concentrated hard enough."

Walter looked at the tiny dragon in her glove. A shiver went up his back.

Pete Santos tapped Walter on the shoulder. He was dressed as a magician. "Guess who I am." Before anyone had a chance to answer he said, "Pete the Magnificent." He lifted his top hat. "Meet the rabbit I pulled out of a hat." His pet goat Homer trotted up beside him wearing big, floppy bunny ears.

"What are *you* supposed to be," Pete asked Walter, "a spy?"

"Detective Dodd at your service." Walter put on his fake nose and mustache and pulled out a magnifying glass.

Johnny Crandall crept up behind Melissa and pretended to bite her neck. She screamed and held her throat. Johnny was dressed as a vampire.

"You're a real pain in the neck," said Melissa.

"That's what all my victims say." Johnny smiled and showed his pointy plastic fangs. Red drops of fake blood dripped down his chin.

"Great costume, Johnny," said Mike.

"Thanks." Johnny swirled his black cape around him. "I come to every game dressed to kill."

Pete laughed. "Want to hear a joke? How do you know a vampire has a cold?"

Everyone shrugged.

"By his *coffin*," said Pete. "Get it?"

Johnny laughed hard. "I've got one too. What did the vampire catch after staying up all night?"

"What?" asked Walter.

"A *bat* cold."

Christy grinned. "That's a very *bat* joke."

Otis walked out of the dugout in a big furry monster suit. He was eating a bag of cookies. "What's so funny?"

"What're *you* supposed to be?" asked Mike.

Otis swallowed. "A cookie monster."

Mike nudged Walter. "I knew he'd find a way to eat and play ball at the same time."

Grandpa Walt walked across the field, hand in hand with a little ghost. He looked

50

fatter around the middle. On his T-shirt was printed: THE SULTAN OF SWAT, BABE RUTH.

"Look!" said Mike. "Coach is Babe Ruth!"

"How'd he get the big stomach?" asked Otis.

Grandpa Walt lifted his shirt. Underneath was a pillow strapped around his waist.

"Guess who I am," said the ghost. Blue eyes looked out from two little holes cut from a white sheet.

"Everyone knows it's you, Jenny," said her big sister, Melissa.

Jenny stamped her feet. "You told!"

Johnny Crandall put an arm around Jenny's shoulder. His black vampire cape draped over her. "You look like part of our team, Jen. Want to switch sides? We could use a little team *spirit*."

Everyone chuckled.

"Enough joking around, kids," said Grandpa Walt. "Let's play ball. Vampires take the field. We're up at bat first. I'm afraid someone's going to have to sit this one out. With Tony's cast off and Mike back, we've got ten players."

"Why can't we all play?" asked Jenny.

"You know the rules," said Grandpa Walt. "Only nine on a team."

"I'll warm the bench," said Tony. He was dressed as his favorite cartoon character—Spiderman. "That'll give me time to work on *Sidelines*." *Sidelines* was the team comic strip.

Jenny stood next to Tony. "I'll sit out too."

"Now *that's* team spirit," said Grandpa Walt. "Jenny can sit out the first half of the game, Tony the second half." Grandpa Walt looked over the batting lineup. "The cookie monster's up first."

Christy and Walter sat down next to each other on the bench. Walter looked out at the field dotted with witch, skeletons, and vampires. "This game is going to be fun," he said.

Christy held her glove up to one ear. "The dragon says my ballet training will win the game."

Walter frowned. "No way. My running will win the game."

Christy smoothed out her pink tutu. "You'll see. Don't forget my dragon helped you find your library book."

Walter looked at the dragon painted inside Christy's baseball glove. It held a tiny baseball in one claw. Fire blazed from its mouth and nose. Walter gulped. He watched Otis set down his cookies and pick up a bat. Otis took quick swings at the first three pitches.

"Strike three!" said the umpire. "You're out!"

Otis looked down at the ground. "Hey, where are my cookies?"

The Vampires' catcher stood up to help Otis look. Crushed beneath his feet were Otis's cookies. "Oops, sorry," he said, peering at Otis through his mummy bandages. "It's hard to see in this costume. I guess that's the way the cookie crumbles."

"Very funny." Otis snatched his package of cookie crumbs and went back to the dugout. "You're up next," he grumbled to Walter.

"Touch the dragon for luck," whispered Christy.

Walter quickly touched the dragon and drew back his hand.

Christy giggled. "It won't bite you, dummy."

Walter's ears burned. "Your dragon's nothing but paint," he said, swinging his Louisville Slugger over his shoulder. He stomped toward the batter's box.

The Vampires' catcher was trying to loosen his mummy costume. "I can't breathe," said the catcher. "My mummy bandage is wrapped too tight."

"I'll help," said Walter. He found the end of the long white bandage and started to wrap it around his wrist.

"Let's play ball!" Johnny yelled from the pitcher's mound. He flung his vampire cape over his shoulder and wound up for the first pitch.

Walter grabbed his bat and swung.
Crack!

Walter stared at the ball sailing over left field. A skeleton, a witch, and a bat scrambled to get beneath it.

"Run!" yelled Melissa from the dugout.

Walter dropped the bat and dashed to first base. He glanced toward the outfield. A skeleton was chasing the ball across the grass. Walter rounded second and headed for third. Something tugged on his arm. The end of the mummy's bandage was still wound around Walter's wrist, and the bandage was being held up by the first- and second-base players!

The Vampires' catcher, Nicky, was spinning round and round, unraveling at home plate as Walter ran the bases.

"Go!" yelled Grandpa Walt. His arms spun around like a windmill. It was the sign to keep running for home.

Walter ran for home plate as the skeleton threw the ball in to Johnny. Johnny turned to throw it home. Nicky didn't even lift his mitt.

The ball bounced against the back fence as Walter ran across home plate.

"Safe!" The umpire called the play and burst out laughing.

Members of the Vampires and the Never Sink Nine were doubled over laughing. Only the Vampires' catcher was quiet. He stood on home plate in his underwear, crying. Tied to his ankle was a long white bandage that trailed around the baseball diamond. The other end of the mummy bandage was wound around Walter's wrist.

Walter jogged back to the red-faced, teary-eyed catcher. "Sorry about your costume," he said.

"I want my mommy," said the catcher.

"Don't you mean your *mummy*?" said Pete from the dugout.

A wave of laughter went through the field.

"If you think you look funny, watch this." Walter took his fake-nose-and-mustache glasses out of his coat pocket and put them

on. The catcher stopped crying and grinned. Then Walter took off his father's trench coat and slipped it over the boy's shoulders. "Here. You wear it. We'll *both* be detectives."

Grandpa Walt jogged onto the field. He put a hand on the catcher's shoulder. "Everything all right over here?"

The catcher and Walter grinned at each other. They both nodded to Grandpa Walt.

Christy was next at bat. She walked up to the plate and took a practice swing. She looked over her shoulder at Walter. "Nice home run, detective. I told you my glove works."

"Maybe," said Walter. He sat down next to Melissa on the dugout bench. She was holding Christy's magic glove.

"Christy said I could hold it," she bragged to Walter.

"Big deal," said Walter, eyeing the glove. He wished she had let him hold it.

Christy bunted to first base. Pete hit her home before the Never Sink Nine had two more outs.

It was the bottom of the first inning and both teams were having a great time. The Never Sink Nine jogged out to their field positions.

The Vampires scored two runs. It was Johnny's turn at bat.

Johnny pretended to flap his wings running to the batter's box. "We vampire bats are batty about batting," he said.

Melissa dug her cowgirl boots into the dirt on the pitcher's mound. She gave her gun holster a pat and wound up the first pitch. "Fire one!" she shouted, and let loose a fast-ball.

Johnny swung too late.

"Strike!" shouted the umpire.

On the second pitch Johnny hit a single. He held out his vampire cape and pretended to fly to first base.

"Next monster," said Melissa from the pitcher's mound.

A tall boy in a monster costume picked up a bat and waited for the pitch.

Mike ran over to Walter on second base. "Watch out," he whispered. "Johnny's trying to steal second."

Mike was right. As Melissa warmed up on the pitcher's mound Johnny quietly crept toward second base.

"Let's have some fun," Mike said to Walter. "Follow me." He pulled out his police whistle and blew it hard. Johnny froze midway between first and second base.

"You're under arrest!" shouted Mike. He ran up to Johnny and handcuffed his hands together.

Johnny looked stunned. "Arrested for what?"

"For stealing," said Mike, loud enough for everyone to hear. "For trying to steal second base!"

Everyone burst out laughing, including Johnny.

Mike gave Johnny a police escort back to first base. He unlocked and slipped off Johnny's handcuffs and warned him not to steal again.

"I promise," said Johnny. As soon as Mike turned around Johnny pretended to bite Mike in the neck with his vampire teeth.

Walter could see Grandpa Walt chuckle from his spot in the Never Sink Nine dugout.

By the bottom of the last inning they were all having so much fun no one knew the score—except Tony. He had been drawing his comic strip in the dugout and keeping track of runs.

"It's Vampires twelve, Never Sink Nine thirteen!" yelled Tony.

Christy, Walter, and Mike walked onto the field together.

"Too bad someone has to lose," said Walter.

"Yeah," said Mike. "But both teams can't win."

Christy held her glove up to one ear and listened. "My dragon says not to worry. He'll take care of everything."

Walter and Mike rolled their eyes at each other as Christy jogged out to center field.

The Vampires were batting. First a black cat and then a monster struck out. Johnny hit a double. When a witch batted Johnny home the score was tied: Never Sink Nine 13, Vampires 13.

"We're tied!" said Walter. Maybe both teams *could* win.

"Not for long," said the witch, standing on second next to Walter. She squinted toward the batter's box. A skeleton was taking a practice swing. "Juan may be a skeleton," she said, "but he's no lazybones. He's our best hitter."

Walter looked over at the outfield. Christy was sitting cross-legged in the middle of the field. She was breathing deeply and her eyes were closed. Felix was blowing his nose in left field and Jenny was pretending to fly around right field in her ghost costume. Homer chased after her.

"We're sunk," Walter said to himself.

Crack! The skeleton hammered a fly ball.

The witch ran for third as the ball sailed over Walter's head to center field.

"Christy!" yelled Walter.

Christy opened her eyes and spotted the ball. She stood up.

"Run for it!" yelled Mike.

"She's too far away," said Walter. "She'll never make it."

Christy started running across the grass. As the ball started falling Christy pushed off. She sprang through the air like a rocket, like a bird, like a ballerina! Her arm reached out and *smack!* The ball plopped into the pocket of her glove.

Christy covered the ball with her free hand and landed in a graceful plié. She smoothed down her tutu and smiled.

"Game!" shouted the umpire. "It's a tie!"

63

Walter's mouth dropped open. Christy's glove *was* magic. It was the perfect game. No one had lost.

The Never Sink Nine cheered and tossed police caps and cowgirl hats into the air. The Vampires flew around the field waving witches' hats and bat wings.

"We won!" both teams yelled.

"The party's at my parents' restaurant!" Christy called out.

"Wait!" said Grandpa Walt, getting out his camera. "Don't forget our team photo." He always took a photo of the Never Sink Nine after each game.

"Can the Vampires be in it too?" asked Walter.

"You bet," said Grandpa Walt.

Both teams crowded into the picture. Walter put on his hat and nose-and-mustache glasses. He squeezed in between Mike and Johnny.

"Say 'Boo,'" said Grandpa Walt.

"Boo!" everyone shouted together as Grandpa Walt took the photo.

"All vampires, ballerinas, and monsters now boarding for the party," said Grandpa Walt.

The two teams began to pile into Grandpa Walt's station wagon and the Vampires' coach's van.

Tony jumped off to one side and started a cheer. "Give a cheer for the Vampires team! Their scary playing is a scream!"

"Yay, Vampires!" yelled the Never Sink Nine.

Johnny Crandall flapped his cape like bat wings. "Here's a cheer for the Never Sink Nine!" he yelled back. "You catch our fly balls every time! We're the bats but you can fly! Your ballerina jumps so high!"

"Yay, Never Sink Nine!" shouted the Vampires.

Grandpa Walt honked his horn. It was time for the costume party.

CHAPTER SEVEN

Friendship First

Christy's parents opened their restaurant early for the costume party. A large dragon kite with a long tail hung over the tables.

"That looks like the dragon on your glove," Walter said to Christy.

"My grandfather brought the kite from China," said Christy.

"I'm starving," said Otis.

"Tell us something new," said Melissa.

Mike and Walter laughed. The entire Never Sink Nine and Vampires teams sat down at a long table. Mr. and Mrs. Chung brought out noodles with sesame sauce and wonton soup. Then everyone shared a dozen different dishes with mounds of rice. Walter was happy they had his favorite—chicken with snow peas.

Mr. and Mrs. Chung made sure everyone felt comfortable eating with chopsticks. It was more fun eating with them than with forks.

Talking about the game stopped when a man with a white beard sat down next to Christy. Christy gave him a hug.

"This is Grandfather Chung," announced Christy.

"The one who painted the magic dragon in your glove?" asked Walter.

Christy and her grandfather smiled at each other.

"You must be Walter," said the old man.

Walter nodded.

"It's nice to see friends playing games and having fun together," said Christy's grandfather. "The Chinese have a saying for sports: friendship first, competition second."

"Couldn't have said it better myself," said Grandpa Walt.

The Chinese are right, thought Walter. Today's was the most fun game the Never Sink Nine had played all season, and no one really cared about winning. The most important thing to concentrate on was having fun—even Mrs. Bumby had known that.

"Want to hear a vampire joke, Mr. Chung?" asked Pete. "Why do vampires brush their teeth?"

Mr. Chung shrugged. "Why?"

"To prevent *bat* breath."

Mr. Chung chuckled.

After everyone finished eating, Christy's parents took down the dragon kite. "The wind's picked up. Why don't you all try it out?"

The two teams ran outside carrying the giant kite. Christy and Otis held up the long tail.

Walter stayed behind to ask Christy's grandfather a question. He was working on a painting by the window. Walter held out his baseball mitt. "Would you make my mitt magic too?"

Mr. Chung smiled. "I can't," he said. "But wait." He dipped his brush in a pot of color and touched the brush to Walter's face. After a few minutes he held up a mirror. Walter looked at his face. A small dragon was painted on his cheek. "Now *you* are magic, Walter."

Walter carefully touched the perfect tiny dragon. "Thanks, Mr. Chung." He ran outside to show it to Christy and the other kids.

He found them in a small park down the street. Vampires and cowgirls, magicians and witches were all running beneath the high-flying kite.

Walter ran over to his grandfather. "Who're we playing next?" he asked.

"It's a surprise," said Grandpa Walt. He lowered the wooden spool of string attached to the kite, and Walter helped hold it.

Walter looked up at the dragon floating through the sky and touched the dragon on his cheek again. He couldn't wait.

About the Author

GIBBS DAVIS was born in Milwaukee, Wisconsin, and was graduated from the University of California at Berkeley. She has published *Swann Song,* a young adult novel, with Avon Books. *Walter's Lucky Socks, Major-League Melissa, Slugger Mike, Pete the Magnificent, Tony's Double Play,* and *Christy's Magic Glove* are all part of the Never Sink Nine series for First Skylark. She divides her time between New York City and Wisconsin.

About the Illustrator

GEORGE ULRICH was born in Morristown, New Jersey, and received his Bachelor of Fine Arts degree from Syracuse University. He has illustrated several Bantam Skylark books, including *Make Four Million Dollars by Next Thursday!* by Stephen Manes and *The Amazing Adventure of Me, Myself, and I* by Jovial Bob Stine. He lives in Marblehead, Massachusetts, with his wife and two sons.